CALICO ILLUSTRATED CLASSICS

Frances Hodgson Burnett's

THE SECRET GARDEN

ADAPTED BY: Jan Fields
ILLUSTRATED BY: Ute Simon

magic
wagon

visit us at www.abdopublishing.com

Published by Magic Wagon, a division of the ABDO Group,
8000 West 78th Street, Edina, Minnesota 55439. Copyright
© 2011 by Abdo Consulting Group, Inc. International copyrights reserved in all countries. All rights reserved. No part of this
book may be reproduced in any form without written permission
from the publisher.

Calico Chapter Books™ is a trademark and logo of Magic Wagon.

Printed in the United States of America, Melrose Park, Illinois.
102010
012011

 This book contains at least 10% recycled materials.

Original text by Frances Hodgson Burnett
Adapted by Jan Fields
Illustrated by Ute Simon
Edited by Stephanie Hedlund and Rochelle Baltzer
Cover and interior design by Abbey Fitzgerald

Library of Congress Cataloging-in-Publication Data

Fields, Jan.
   The secret garden / Frances Hodgson Burnett ; adapted by Jan Fields ;
illustrated by Ute Simon.
      p. cm. -- (Calico illustrated classics)
   ISBN 978-1-61641-108-4
   [1. Orphans--Fiction. 2. Gardens--Fiction. 3. People with disabilities--
Fiction 4. Yorkshire (England)--History--20th century--Fiction. 5.
Great Britain--History--Edward VII, 1901-1910--Fiction.] I. Simon, Ute,
ill. II. Burnett, Frances Hodgson, 1849-1924. Secret garden. III. Title.
   PZ7.F479177Se 2011
   [Fic]--dc22
                              2010031049

Table of Contents

There Is No One Left

Mary Lennox had a little thin face and a little thin body. Her yellow hair hung limp and dull. Her skin was faintly yellow and she wore a tight, sour expression at all times.

She was born in India, squalling, thin and ugly. Her pretty mother took one look at her and said that she must be kept out of sight. Mary was handed over to a servant, and her mother rarely looked upon her again.

For nine years, Mary's life rarely changed. Then one frightfully hot morning, she awoke feeling very cross. She sat up to snap at her nursemaid, only to see a strange servant standing beside her bed.

"Why are you there?" she demanded. "Send my Ayah to me now!"

The stranger looked frightened and stammered, "I sorry, Missie Sahib. Your Ayah cannot come."

Mary shrieked, slapped, and kicked as the strange woman tried to help her dress. The stranger left the room as quickly as she could.

Mary stormed around the house. None of the servants would tell her anything about her Ayah. They merely hurried away when they spotted her.

Finally, Mary wandered out into the garden and began to play by herself near the veranda. Mary pretended she was making a flower bed. She picked blossoms from the tall hibiscus hedge and stuck the red flowers into little heaps of dirt.

Mary heard her mother come out on the veranda with a fair young officer. The two spoke together in low voices. Mary stared at her mother, since she got so few glimpses of her. She was a tall, slim, pretty person who wore such lovely clothes and seemed always to be laughing or smiling.

Now her eyes were large and scared. "Is it so very bad?" she asked. "Oh, is it?"

"Awfully," the young man said and Mary heard his voice tremble. "You ought to have gone to the hills two weeks ago."

Mary's mother wrung her hands. "I only stayed to go to a silly dinner party!" she cried. "What a fool I was!"

While Mary puzzled over what her mother meant, wailing rang out from the servants' quarters. Mary's mother clutched the young officer's arm. Mary stood up, shivering as the wailing grew wilder and wilder.

"What is it?" her mother cried.

"Someone has died," the young officer said. "You didn't say the sickness had broken out here!"

"I didn't know," Mrs. Lennox gasped. She turned and ran into the house with the young officer at her heels.

Eventually someone explained to Mary that a terrible sickness was killing people. Ayah was the first of the household to die, but the wailing sounded throughout the house over and over.

In the confusion and the sickness, Mary hid herself in her nursery. She was soon completely forgotten. No one came to her or brought her food or news.

Once she crept out into the dining room and found the table set with food but no one there. She ate some fruit and biscuits and wandered back to her room to sleep away the hours until someone would remember her again.

When she awakened, the house was silent. No one wailed. No one rushed past her door. *Maybe everyone has gotten well,* she thought. Maybe someone would remember her and bring her food and a cool drink. But no one came.

Mary soon heard something rustling. When she looked down, she saw a small, harmless snake crawling across the matting on her floor.

"How queer and quiet it is," she told him.

He slipped out under her door as she watched. Suddenly Mary heard men's footsteps. Low voices sounded outside her door and she crept closer to hear.

"What desolation," one man said. "That pretty, pretty woman. I heard there was a child too, though no one ever saw her."

Mary glared at the door and it opened. The officer who looked in was so startled at the sight of her that he jumped back. "Mercy, a child! In a place like this!"

Mary frowned at the officer and said, "I am Mary Lennox. I fell asleep while everyone was sick. Why does no one come?"

"It's the child no one saw," a second officer said as men crowded around the door. "She was actually forgotten."

"Poor little kid," a kind-looking man said. "There is nobody left to come."

And so Mary learned that her father and mother were dead. Any servants left alive had fled, and she was alone in the world.

Mistress Mary Quite Contrary

For a time, Mary lived with an English clergyman nearby. He had five children in shabby clothes who quarreled constantly. Their house was never clean and Mary spent most of her time alone outside, snarling whenever another child would come to tease her.

Everyone seemed relieved when Mary's uncle was discovered in England. She learned of it from the clergyman's son Basil.

"I heard Father and Mother talking about your uncle," he said. "He lives in a big, old house in the country. No one goes near him. He's so cross he won't let them, and they wouldn't come if he did let them. He's a hunchback, and he's horrid."

"I don't believe you," Mary said. She turned her back and stuck her fingers in her ears. She would not listen to any more.

"He's as horrid as you!" Basil danced around her and sang, "Mistress Mary Quite Contrary!"

Basil's mother confirmed that Mary would be going to live with her uncle. Mary made the long voyage to England under the care of an officer's wife.

Although Mary threw no tantrums during the voyage, the young wife was happy to hand her over to the woman Mr. Archibald Craven had sent to meet her in London. Mary's cross little face and cold speech had made the trip quite gloomy.

Mary looked up at her new caretaker. She was a stout woman with very red cheeks and sharp, black eyes. She wore a purple dress, a black silk mantle with fringes, and a black bonnet with a purple velvet flower that trembled when the woman moved her head.

"I am Mrs. Medlock," the woman said. "I am the housekeeper for Mr. Craven."

Mary merely nodded coldly. She felt Mrs. Medlock was disagreeable and common, so she tried to walk a bit apart from her so no one would think they were together.

In the railway carriage, Mary sat silently with her thin, black-gloved hands folded in her lap. Her black dress and hat made Mary's skin look yellower than ever.

Mrs. Medlock watched her for a while, then said, "I suppose I may as well tell you something about where you are going. Did your father and mother tell you much about your uncle?"

"No," said Mary, frowning as she tried to remember her father or mother ever telling her anything at all.

"You are going to an odd place," Mrs. Medlock said. "The house is 600 years old and it's grand, but gloomy. There's near a hundred rooms in it, though most are not used. There's a big park around it but nothing else."

Mary had found herself interested. The house sounded nothing like India. But when the woman stopped talking, Mary only sat silently.

"Eh," Mrs. Medlock said. "What do you think of it?"

"It doesn't matter," said Mary. "I will be going there whatever I think."

"You are right enough there," said Mrs. Medlock. "Your uncle won't trouble himself about you. He never troubles himself about

no one. He's got a crooked back and he's been sour all his life except when he was married."

Mary's eyes widened. She never thought about her uncle being married.

"She was a sweet, pretty thing and he'd have given her the world," the woman said, clearly warming to her subject now that Mary had shown a bit of interest. "It broke him when she died."

Mary gave an involuntary jump. "Oh, she died?" she said. She had loved the idea of her pretty aunt loving a man with a crooked back. It was like something from a fairy tale. But now her aunt was gone and that did not make Mary feel cheerful.

"Yes. Now your uncle sees no one and he won't see you," she said. "You may play in the gardens but don't go poking around the house."

"I won't go poking around," Mary said. Then she turned her face toward the window of the railway carriage and watched the rain run down the panes until she fell asleep.

Across the Moor

Mary slept a long time. It was quite dark when the train stopped at a station and Mrs. Medlock shook her.

"You have had a sleep," Mrs. Medlock said. "We're at Thwaite Station, and we've a long drive ahead of us."

The station was small and nobody else seemed to be getting out of the train. The stationmaster nodded to Mrs. Medlock in a good-natured way.

A carriage stood on the road before the little outside platform. A neatly dressed footman helped Mary climb aboard. His long waterproof coat shone and dripped with rain.

Mary was seated in a comfortable cushioned corner. She was curious to see something of the road over which she was driven. The carriage lamps cast rays of light a little distance ahead of them. They drove through a tiny village, then onto a high road. She saw hedges and trees.

Finally the horses began to go more slowly, as if climbing uphill. Mary could see no more trees or hedges. In fact, she saw nothing but darkness. She pressed her face against the window.

"We're on the moor now sure enough," said Mrs. Medlock.

A great expanse of dark spread out around them. The wind made a wild, low rushing sound.

"Is it the sea?" Mary asked.

"No. Nor is it fields or mountains. It's miles and miles of wild land."

"It sounds like the sea," Mary murmured.

"That's the wind blowing through the bushes," Mrs. Medlock said. "This is a wild place, though there are plenty who like it."

Mary frowned. "I don't like it," she whispered too low for the woman to hear.

Eventually the carriage passed through the park gates of the estate. The trees on either side of the road made it seem like they drove through a long vault. Finally they reached a clear spot and Mary glimpsed the hugely long, low-built house. The house seemed to ramble round a stone court.

The carriage halted at the entrance door and Mary felt small and lost against its huge size. A neat, thin old man stood near the door.

"You are to take her to her rooms," he said. "He doesn't want to see her. He's leaving for London in the morning."

"Very well, Mr. Pritcher," Mrs. Medlock said. She led Mary up a broad staircase, down a long corridor, and then through another and another. Finally, Mary found herself in a room with a fire in it and a supper on the table.

"Well, here you are. This room and the next are where you'll live," Mrs. Medlock said. "You must keep to them." Then she left Mary alone.

Mary never felt quite so contrary in her life.

CHAPTER 4

Martha

When Mary opened her eyes in the morning, a young housemaid was kneeling on the hearth-rug raking out the cinders noisily. Mary lay and watched her for a few moments before looking around the room. Through an open window, she saw a great stretch of land that looked like an endless purple sea without trees.

"What is that?" she asked, pointing out the window.

The young housemaid looked and answered with a grin. "That's the moor. Do you like it?"

"No," Mary said simply. "I hate it."

"That's because you're not used to it." Martha turned back to polish away at the grate cheerfully. She said, "But you'll like it."

"Do you?" Mary asked.

"Aye, I love it. It's fair lovely in the spring."

Mary puzzled over the cheery young servant who spoke to her as if they were equals. She thought of the times she'd slapped her Ayah and decided that if she slapped this young woman, she'd likely be slapped back.

"You're a strange servant," Mary said finally.

"Eh, I know that," the girl replied. "If there was a grand missus at Misselthwaite, I am certain I'd not have a job at all. But the master cares nothing about servants and my mother is great friends with Mrs. Medlock."

"What's your name? Are you going to be my servant?" Mary asked.

"I'm Martha and I'm Mrs. Medlock's servant," she said. "But I'm to wait on you a bit. Though you won't need much waiting on."

"Who is going to dress me?" Mary asked.

"A great big thing like you?" Martha said in surprise. "Can't you dress yourself?"

"I never have."

"Then it's time you should learn."

At that, Mary felt such a wave of frustration and oddness that she burst into tears.

"Eh! You mustn't cry like that," Martha said, rushing to Mary's side. "I beg your pardon, Miss. Do stop crying."

Martha's friendly tone helped calm Mary. Soon her sobs died down to sniffles.

"I'll help you with your clothes a bit if you get out of bed," Martha said. "And then you must eat your breakfast."

Mary was surprised to find she had a pretty new dress in soft white wool. Martha explained that Mr. Craven didn't want her to make the place sadder than it already was by wandering around in black.

"I hate black things," Mary agreed.

It took some work to get Mary into her new clothes. She'd been used to being dressed like a doll but Martha insisted she do most of her own changing.

As Mary dressed, Martha chattered about her own family. She had eleven brothers and

sisters. Mary found Martha's brother Dickon especially interesting.

"He's twelve years old," Martha explained. "And he's got a young pony he calls Jump."

"Where did he get it?" Mary asked. She'd never had a pet of her own and the thought of a pony seemed quite wonderful.

"He found it on the moor with its mother. He made friends with it, and it got to like him so much it follows him like a pup. He even rides it."

After that, Martha led Mary to the next room for breakfast. Mary barely picked at it as she was rarely hungry. Martha was indignant to see so much food wasted, so finally Mary ate a little toast and marmalade.

When she finished, Martha shook her head over the waste but merely said, "You wrap up warm and run out to play in the garden. It will do you good and give you a bit of an appetite, too."

Mary looked out the window. "It looks cold. Why would I go out in the cold?"

"Well, if you don't go out, you'll have to stay in. What have you to do in here?" Martha asked.

Mary glanced around her. The room held neither toys nor books. "Who will go with me?" she asked.

"You'll go by yourself," Martha answered. "Our Dickon goes off on the moor by himself for hours and makes friends with every creature he finds."

At the mention of Dickon, Mary decided to go out.

"There are many gardens," Martha said as she directed Mary on how to get out to them. "But one is locked up and no one has been in it for ten years."

"Why?"

"It was Mrs. Craven's favorite garden," Martha said sadly. "Mr. Craven shut it up when she died ten years ago. He even buried the key. No one can get inside."

At that, Mary's curiosity woke up. She decided she would find this secret garden as quickly she could.

Ben and the Robin

Mary wandered through the many paths of the gardens. She wondered what the secret garden would be like and whether any flowers could live in a place shut up for ten years.

She went through an open door into yet another section of the garden and found beds for vegetables and fruit trees. There was nothing pretty about the cold, lifeless beds in winter.

Presently an old man with a spade walked through the door to this walled garden. He had a surly old face and glared at her. Mary merely glared back more fiercely.

"What is this place?" she asked.

"Kitchen garden," he answered, then he grunted and pointed to a far wall. "There's more beyond."

"Can I go there?" Mary asked.

"If you like, but there's nothing to see."

Mary didn't answer but wandered on through several enclosed gardens. Then she saw a wall with a bird perched on it watching her. The tiny bird had a bright red chest. When he saw her looking, he burst into song.

Mary found she liked him very much.

"Ah, you've met the cheeky little beggar," a gruff voice said. It was the old man from the kitchen garden, now with a slight smile for the bird. He spoke to the bird, "You must be courting to be out so early in the season."

"What kind of bird is he?" Mary asked. "He seems so tame."

"He's a robin redbreast and they're the friendliest of birds. And that one is more curious than all the others," he said with a chuckle. "And he likes folks to talk about him."

The bird seemed pleased. He flew right down to peck at the ground near the old man's feet.

"What's your name?" Mary asked the old man.

"Ben Weatherstaff," he answered. "And you're the little girl from India." Then he chuckled again. "We've got a good bit in common. We're both plain as a boot and sour as we look. And we've got the same friend now," he said gesturing toward the robin.

Mary looked at the robin and spoke in a soft tone. "Would you make friends with me?" The bird looked at her in a friendly way, then ruffled his feathers and flew back over the wall.

"Where does that go?" she asked. "Where is the door to go there?"

"He lives in a garden there," Ben said. "And there's no door that you can find, and none that's any of your business. Get you gone and play now."

Then the old man threw the spade over his shoulder and walked off without another glance or a good-bye.

The Cry in the Corridor

At first, each day passed for Mary Lennox exactly like the day before. She awoke and chatted with Martha. Then she went out and wandered the gardens, always finding something interesting.

After a few days spent almost entirely out of doors, she awakened one morning hungry. She cheerfully ate up her porridge.

"The air of the moor is giving you an appetite," Martha said with approval.

As Mary wandered the gardens, she chattered often at the little robin. He appeared whenever Mary grew close to the walls that she knew hid the secret garden from her. The cheerful little bird always made her smile.

Her search for a way into the mysterious garden kept her out of doors every day. She came in only for meals. She was almost never cross with Martha and loved hearing stories of Martha's big family crowded together for lively fun in their small cottage. Martha seemed to like having an audience for her stories and often lingered with Mary.

"Listen to the wind wuthering around the house," Martha said one night.

Mary wasn't sure what "wuthering" meant, but she could hear the hollow, shuddering sort of roar. It rushed round and round the house. As Mary listened, she heard an odd sound mixed with the roar of the wind.

"Do you hear anyone crying?" she asked.

Martha looked up, startled. "No. It's the wind."

"Listen," Mary insisted. "It's coming from inside the house." Suddenly the sound grew louder as if someone had opened a door to the crying child.

"There, I told you so. It is someone crying!" Mary said.

Martha stood up fiercely. "It was the wind," she said. "And if it wasn't, it was just the scullery maid. She has a toothache."

Martha rushed off soon after and Mary knew that Martha had lied to her for some reason.

The next morning, Mary couldn't go outside at all because a great storm still raged. She decided to go wandering a bit inside the house. She knew Mrs. Medlock wouldn't like it, but she wasn't a bit afraid of the grumpy woman.

As Mary wandered, she found doors and doors and corridors and corridors. It was exactly like wandering through the twists and turns of the garden, only indoors.

Some of the doors were locked, but many were not. Mary found rooms of fine furniture and walls filled with paintings. The people from the paintings stared down at her as if they wondered what a little girl from India was doing in their house.

In one room, she found shelves filled with little ivory elephants and she played with them for a quite a long time. In another room, she found a velvet cushion with a great hole in it. When Mary peered in, she saw black eyes peering out. A mouse had made the cushion her nest, where she tended her six babies.

Finally, Mary grew fiercely hungry and headed back to her rooms. As she drew closer, she paused. She heard crying again.

"It is someone," she whispered. "I knew there was." And Mary decided she *would* find out where this mysterious child was shut up to cry.

The Key of the Garden

Two days after this, Mary opened her eyes and sat upright in bed. She said, "Look at the moor! Look at the moor!"

The rainstorm had ended and the gray mist and clouds had been swept away by the night and the wind. A deep blue sky arched high over the moor. Never had Mary dreamed of a sky so blue. In India, skies were hot and blazing. This was a deep, cool blue like a lovely bottomless lake.

"The storm is over for a bit," said Martha with a cheerful grin. "It does that this time of year because springtime is on its way. It's a long way off yet, but it is coming."

"I thought it always rained or looked dark in England," Mary said.

"No, it's bright and beautiful in the spring," said Martha, sitting up on her heels near the hearth. "You'll want to live on the moor all day like Dickon does."

"I would like that," Mary said wistfully. "I would like to see your cottage and I would like to meet Dickon. I like Dickon, and I've never seen him."

"Well," said Martha stoutly, "I wonder what Dickon would think of you."

"He wouldn't like me," Mary said in her stiff, cold little way. "No one likes me."

Martha looked at her thoughtfully, then asked as if she were really curious, "How do you like yourself?"

Mary thought it over. "Not at all really. But I never thought of that before."

Martha grinned a little and went away in high spirits as soon as she had given Mary her breakfast. It was Martha's afternoon off and she was going to walk five miles across the moor to the cottage. She was going to help her mother with the washing and do the week's baking and enjoy herself thoroughly.

Mary went out into the garden. The first thing she did was run round and round the fountain flower garden ten times. She counted the times carefully and when she was finished she felt better and less alone. She went into the first kitchen garden and found Ben working there with the two other gardeners.

"Springtime's coming," he said. "Can you smell it?"

Mary sniffed and thought she could.

"You'll see bits of green spikes poking out of the black earth soon."

"What will they be?" Mary asked.

"Crocus and snowdrops and daffydowndillys. Have you never seen them?"

"No," Mary said. "Everything is wet and green after the rains in India. I think it all grows up in a night."

"It won't grow up so fast here. You'll have to wait for them. They'll poke up a bit higher every day. They'll push out a spike here and there. They'll uncurl a leaf this day and that. You watch."

"I'll watch." Mary walked away thinking. She had begun to like the garden. She had begun to like the robin and Dickon and even Ben. She was beginning to like Martha, too. That seemed a good many people to like when you aren't used to liking anyone.

As she walked, she heard a chirp and a twitter. She looked at the bare flower bed on her left side and there was the robin. He hopped about and pretended to peck at things.

"Do you remember me?" Mary cried. "You do. You are prettier than anything else in the world."

In the flower bed, the earth had been turned up because a dog had been trying to dig up a mole. Mary looked into the hole. She saw something almost buried in the dirt. It looked like a rusty ring. When she picked it up, it was an old key.

Mary stood and stared at it as it hung from her finger. "It's the key to the secret garden," she whispered.

Mary looked at the key for quite a long time. She put it in her pocket and walked slowly along the ivy-draped wall. The ivy was a baffling thing. Howsoever carefully she looked, she could see nothing but thickly growing glossy dark green leaves. She had the key now, but where was the door?

The Robin Who Showed the Way

Martha was back at work in the morning, her cheeks redder than ever and in the best of spirits. She was full of stories of the delights of being home with her family.

"They did like to hear about you," said Martha. "They also had a million questions about the people of India. I couldn't tell them enough."

"I'll tell you a great deal more before your next day out," Mary said, "so you will have more to talk about. I dare say they would like to hear about riding on elephants and camels."

"My word!" cried a delighted Martha. "That would set them clean off their heads. Would you really do that, Miss?"

Mary nodded solemnly. "Did Dickon like hearing about me?"

"His eyes nearly started out of his head, they got that round," answered Martha. "But Mother worried about you being all alone so much. She told me I should do my best to cheer you up."

"You do cheer me up," Mary said. "I like to hear you talk."

Suddenly Martha hurried out of the room and returned with something held behind her back. "I've brought you a present."

"A present!"

"A peddler came by our door and Elizabeth Ellen saw that he had a skipping rope with a red and blue handle. Mother thought it was just the thing for you. It'll make you strong."

"What do I do with it?" Mary asked curiously.

"Do they not have skipping ropes in India?" Martha cried out. "Watch me and I'll show you what it's for."

Martha ran to the middle of the room. She took a handle in each hand and began to skip and skip and skip. Mary stared at her and the odd faces in the portrait seemed to stare at her as well. But Martha did not even see them. She went on skipping and counting as she skipped until she reached a hundred.

"I could skip longer than that when I was twelve," she said. "But I wasn't as fat then as I am now. And I practiced."

Mary got up from her chair nearly bursting with excitement. "Do you think I could ever skip like that?"

"You just try," Martha said. "You'll skip a little more each time you try."

"Thank you, thank you." Mary raced outside with the skipping rope. She was not very clever with it at first, but she liked it so much she didn't want to stop.

Mary counted and skipped until her cheeks were quite red. She skipped around all the gardens and round the orchard. Before she got halfway down the path near the wall to the secret garden, she saw the robin swaying on a long branch of ivy.

"You showed me where the key was yesterday," she said, skipping to stop. "You ought to show me the door today. But I don't believe you know where it is."

The robin flew from his swinging spray of ivy to the top of the wall. He opened his beak and sang a loud trill, just to show off. One of the little gusts of wind rushed down the walk. It was strong enough to wave the branches of the trees, and it was more than strong enough to swing the bit of ivy hanging from the wall.

Mary jumped toward the wall. This she did because she had seen something under the ivy. A round knob was covered by the leaves hanging over it. It was the knob of a door!

She put her hands under the leaves to pull and push them aside. The ivy was a loose and swinging curtain. The robin kept singing and twittering away as if he were as excited as she was. Mary found the lock of the door.

Mary put her hand in her pocket and drew out the key. It fit the keyhole perfectly. It took two hands to turn the key in the rusty lock, but it did turn.

Mary looked up and down the walk. No one was coming. No one would know. She opened the door slowly and slipped through it, closing it behind her. She was standing inside the secret garden.

The Strangest House

Inside the garden, the high walls were covered with leafless stems of climbing roses. They were so thick they had matted together. Clumps of rosebushes had grown and spread their branches until they were like little trees. Climbing roses crept up every tree in the garden. They ran all over them and swung down long tendrils like swaying curtains.

"How still it is," Mary whispered. She could not tell what was alive and what was dead because everything was winter brown.

The robin had flown to his treetop. He did not even flutter his wings as he looked at Mary.

"I am the first person who has spoken in here for ten years," she said.

Mary stepped as softly as if she were afraid of awakening someone. She walked under the fairylike arches between the trees. She looked up at the sprays and tendrils that formed the arches.

"I hope you aren't dead," she whispered.

She felt as if she had found a world all her own. Finally the robin flew down from his treetop and hopped about from one bush to another. He chirped a good deal as if he were showing her things.

Mary's skipping rope hung over her arm and after she walked for a while, she thought she would skip around the whole garden. And so she skipped, stopping now and again to look at things.

Finally she came to an alcove that had once had a flower bed in it, and she thought she saw something sticking out of the black earth. She knelt down to look.

"Yes, they are tiny growing things and they might be crocuses or snowdrops or daffodils,"

she said, remembering what Ben had told her. "It isn't quite a dead garden after all."

Mary did not know anything about gardening, but the grass seemed so thick she worried that the new shoots had no place to grow. She searched about until she found a rather sharp piece of wood, and dug out the weeds and grass until she made a nice clear place for the young shoots.

Tired and cheerful, she finally stopped. "I will come back this afternoon," she said, looking around at her new kingdom. Then she ran lightly across the grass and slipped through the door.

She had such red cheeks and such bright eyes and ate so much dinner that Martha was delighted.

"Does Dickon know about flowers and plants and growing things?" Mary asked.

"Our Dickon can make a flower grow out of a brick wall," Martha said loyally.

"I wish spring were here now so I could see all the things that grow in England," Mary said. "I wish, I wish I had a little spade."

"What do you want a spade for?" Martha asked, laughing.

"I thought if I had a little spade, I might make a little garden if Ben would give me some seeds."

Martha's face lit up. "Why that's the very thing mother said. She said you would enjoy planting a bit of things for yourself, and that it would be good for you to watch them grow."

"Your mother knows so many things," Mary said. "How much would a spade cost?"

"At Thwaite village there's a shop that has a spade and a rake and a fork, all tied together for two shillings," Martha said.

"I have more than that in my purse," said Mary. "Mrs. Medlock gave me some money from Mr. Craven. She said I'm to have an allowance every week. I've had nothing to spend it on so far, but now I do."

"That shop also sells seeds and we can have Dickon pick out the prettiest ones and the easiest to grow," Martha said. "We can give him the note with the money and the things you want to buy."

"How will I get the things when Dickon buys them?"

"He'll bring them to you himself. He likes to walk this way, and I know he'd like to meet you."

Mary was so happy at the thought of the gardening tools and seeds that she nearly forgot the question she meant to ask. "Martha," she said, "has the maid had the toothache again today?"

"What makes you ask?"

"When I was coming in to eat, I walked down the corridor and I heard that far-off crying again. There isn't a wind today so I wondered if it might be the maid."

"You must not walk in the corridors alone," Martha said, her eyes round. "Mr. Craven would be angry. Now I hear Mrs. Medlock's bell, and I must be going."

As Martha rushed out of the room, Mary frowned. She was certain no bell had rung.

"This is the strangest house anyone has ever lived in," she said drowsily. Then she dropped her head on the cushioned seat of the armchair and fell asleep.

Dickon

The sun shone down for nearly a week in the secret garden. Mary loved the feeling that when the beautiful walls shut her in, no one knew where she was. It reminded her of the fairy storybook she'd read. She felt wider awake every day that passed.

Mary worked and pulled the weeds steadily, becoming more pleased with her work every hour. She found many more of the sprouting green and pale points than she'd ever hoped to find. They seemed to be starting everywhere.

Several times she found Ben working in the main gardens and asked him questions about plants.

"You're like that robin," he said to her one morning when he lifted his head to find her standing by him. "I never know when I shall see you or which side you'll come from. How long have you lived here now?"

"I think it's been about a month," she answered.

"You do the place credit," he said. "You're bigger than you were, and not a bit of yellow to your skin. You looked a bit like a plucked crow first I saw you."

"My stockings are getting tighter," Mary said. "They used to make wrinkles."

Then the robin fluttered down to show off a bit for Ben, flying right over and landing on the handle of Ben's shovel.

"There you are," he said. "I know what you're up to. You're courting some pretty young miss."

After a bit, Ben grumbled that he needed to get back to his work and sent Mary on her way. She skipped slowly down the outside wall and thought of how much she liked old Ben.

Finally she reached the gate that opened into a wood. She saw a boy sitting under a tree where a brown squirrel was clinging and watching him. Quite nearby, two rabbits sat up and sniffed with twitching noses. All the while, the boy played a song on a rough wooden flute.

When he saw Mary, he held up a hand and spoke softly, "Don't move or they'll be frightened away."

Mary stood very still while the boy finished the tune on his flute. He stood slowly to his feet, and the creatures scampered away in no great hurry.

"I'm Dickon," he said. "And you are Miss Mary."

"Did you get our note?" she asked.

He nodded, and his rusty curls shook. "That's why I'm here." He handed her a packet that held a little spade, a rake, and a hoe.

"They're good tools. And the woman in the shop threw in a packet of white poppy seeds and one of blue larkspur when I bought the other seeds."

Mary and Dickon sat together on a log and looked at the bundle of small packages. A picture of a flower was pasted to the front of each one. Dickon explained what the flowers were and what they liked and how best to grow them. Mary soon quite forgot to feel shy around the friendly boy.

Suddenly, he stopped speaking and turned his head quickly. "Where's the robin that is calling us?" he asked.

"It's old Ben's robin, but I think he knows me a little."

"Aye, he knows you. And he likes you," Dickon said.

"Do you understand everything birds say?" Mary asked.

Dickon laughed. "I think maybe I do. So tell me, where is your garden? We can start the planting."

Mary's thin hands clutched each other as they lay in her lap. She didn't know if she should tell this boy her secret.

"I don't know anything about boys," she said. "Can you keep a secret?"

"I keep the secret of every bird's nest and every rabbit's nest and every newborn in the moor," he said looking puzzled. "I can keep a secret."

Mary put out her hand and clutched his sleeve. "I've taken a garden that no one wanted. They're letting it die, all shut up by itself. I found it and I got into it with the help of the robin."

"Where is it?" Dickon whispered.

Mary got up from the log. She led him round the laurel path into the walk where the ivy grew thick. She lifted the hanging ivy and pushed open the door.

Dickon looked round and round about him. Finally he whispered, "It's like being in a dream."

Might I Have a Bit of Earth?

Dickon and Mary walked around the secret garden. He showed her which of the roses still lived and which had died. He trimmed back the dead growth to make more room for the new growth that would come on in the spring.

Mary showed Dickon all of the small green sprouts she had found. He told her which flowers would grow from them. He praised her work as a gardener.

"I thought you didn't know a thing about gardening," he said in surprise. "But this is done just right."

"They were so little, and the grass was so thick and strong," Mary said. "I just tried to make a place for them."

"A gardener could not have done it better."

"Will you come and help me to do the things the garden needs?" Mary asked.

"I'll come every day if you like," Dickon said. "I'll help you wake up the garden."

"You are as nice as Martha said you were," Mary said, seriously. "I like you, and you make the fifth person. I never thought I would like five people."

Dickon sat back on his heels where he was pulling weeds and looked at her. "Who are the other four?" he asked with a laugh.

"Your mother and Martha and the robin and Ben." Mary counted them off on her fingers as she spoke. "I'm counting the robin because Ben says he thinks he's a person."

Dickon laughed so hard at that, they had to cover his mouth so no one would hear. Then he looked up at the sky and said, "It's time for your noon meal. I'll keep working here, and you go in and eat. We can meet in the garden again tomorrow."

Mary ran to the house so fast that her hair was ruffled on her forehead and her cheeks were bright pink. Her dinner sat on the table and Martha stood beside it.

"I've seen Dickon," Mary gasped. "He's teaching me wonderful things about plants."

"Now you just need your own garden," Martha said as Mary sat down to eat. Mary ate as quickly as she could and jumped up to put on her hat and go back outside. But Martha stopped her.

"Mr. Craven wants to see you as soon as you're done with your meal," Martha said.

Mary turned quite pale. The door opened and Mrs. Medlock walked in. "Your hair is rough," she announced. "You must brush it and put on your best dress."

After Mary was made tidy, she was taken to a part of the house she'd never seen before. Mrs. Medlock knocked on a closed door and someone said, "Come in." They entered the room together.

Inside, Mary saw a man sitting in the armchair before the fire.

"This is Miss Mary, sir," Mrs. Medlock said.

"You may leave her. I will ring for you when I want you to take her away."

Mary twisted her thin hands together nervously as Mrs. Medlock left. She could see Mr. Craven had a twisted back and his black hair was streaked with white. She thought he had the saddest face she'd ever seen.

"Come here," he said. "Are you well? You're very thin."

"I am getting fatter," Mary answered.

"I meant to get you a nurse or governess but I forgot," he said.

"I'm too big for a nurse," Mary said. "Please don't give me a governess yet. I want to play out of doors. It is making me stronger and well."

"That is what Martha's mother said. She stopped me in the street to say it," he muttered absentmindedly.

"She knows a lot about children," said Mary. "She has twelve. She knows. Martha's mother sent me a skipping rope. I skip and run and look for things that are sprouting in the gardens. I don't do any harm."

"Don't look so frightened," he said in a worried voice. "What harm could be in a child like you? You may do as you like." He looked at her for a few moments, then suddenly asked, "Do you want toys, books, or dolls?"

"Could I have a bit of earth to garden?" she asked, her voice trembling.

"Do you like gardens very much? You can have as much earth as you want," he said. "You remind me of someone else who loved the earth and things that grow. If you see any bit of garden that you want, take it and make it come alive."

"From anywhere that's not wanted?" Mary asked.

"Anywhere at all," he said. "But you must go now because I'm tired." He rang the bell for Mrs. Medlock and told her that Mary must be allowed to play and run free and not to look after her too much. He said Martha's mother might visit sometime. Mrs. Medlock was especially pleased with the idea of not looking after Mary too much.

"Thank you, sir," Mrs. Medlock said.

Mary danced back to her room. She told Martha what he had said and Martha agreed that Mr. Craven truly was a nice man, only so very sad.

Mary put on her hat to rush back outside. When she reached the secret garden, Dickon was gone. Stuck on a thorn in the rosebush was a scrap of paper. It read, "I will come back."

CHAPTER 12

I Am Colin

That night, Mary fell asleep dreaming of the secret garden. But night blew in a storm that poured down and woke Mary. She listened miserably to the wind roaring around the house.

"The rain knew I didn't want it," she grumbled. "And so it came."

Suddenly she recognized another sound in the house. She slipped out of bed and tiptoed to her door. "It's someone crying, I know it is."

Mary took up the candle from beside her bed and went softly into the corridor. Though the halls were very dark, Mary was so filled with curiosity, she barely noticed. She passed through hall after hall and door after door, following the sound.

Finally, Mary knew she stood right outside the source of the crying. Someone was crying on the other side of the door, and it was quite a young someone.

She pushed open the door and went into a big room. A low fire glowed in the hearth. A four-posted bed hung with brocade held a boy. He was crying pitifully. The boy had ivory skin and delicate features with eyes that seemed too big for his face. He had a lot of dark hair that tumbled across his forehead.

Mary crept closer and the boy stared at her, his eyes growing even larger, "Who are you?" he whispered. "Are you a ghost?"

"No," Mary whispered back. "Are you?"

He stared and stared and finally shook his head. "I am Colin Craven. Who are you?"

"I am Mary Lennox. Mr. Craven is my uncle."

"He is my father," the boy said.

Mary gasped. No one told her that her uncle had a son. Why didn't they tell her?

Colin reached out and touched her. "You are real," he said. "I have such real dreams sometimes. I thought you were a dream."

"Why were you crying?" Mary asked.

"Because I couldn't go to sleep and my head ached," he said. "No one told me you were here."

"I wonder why," Mary said.

"I don't let people see me," he said. "I may be a hunchback and I'm not going to live. That's why my father never comes to see me, except when he thinks I'm asleep. My mother died when I was born. He almost hates me."

Mary peered closely at the boy. "You don't look at all like a hunchback. Have you always been here?"

"Nearly always. I don't like to go out because people stare. I used to wear an iron thing to keep my back straight, but a doctor in London said it was stupid. He made them take it off. He said I should go out in the fresh air in this wheeled chair, but I won't! I hate fresh air and I hate people. I don't want anyone to look at me."

"I didn't like the air when I first came here," Mary said. "But if you don't like people to see you, do you want me to go away?"

"No, I want you to stay and talk to me," he said. So Mary put her candle on the table and sat down near him. She asked what he would like her to talk about. He asked questions about her and about why she was at Misselthwaite. She answered everything he asked.

Finally he asked, "How old are you?"

"I am ten and so are you," she said. "You were born when the secret garden was shut up ten years ago."

Colin's eyes grew wide and he asked about the garden. Mary told him everything she knew, except that she had the key and had been inside. She wasn't sure yet if Colin was the kind of boy who could keep a secret.

"I would love to see a secret garden," he said sleepily. "I will have someone find the key and let us into the garden."

"And will they do it?" she asked.

"They do anything I say," he answered. "If I weren't going to die, I would be master here someday."

"Are you so sure you will die?" Mary asked.

"I've heard them whisper about it. But I don't want to talk about that. Tell me what you think is in the garden."

And so Mary described the bulbs pushing shoots just out of the soil, green and thin. She told him about the roses that made curtains in the trees and looked dead but weren't. She told him about the animals who hid in the secret garden because it was safe and still.

"You make it sound like you've seen it," he said. "I think I could get well in a garden like that."

"Perhaps I can find out how to get into the garden some day," Mary said. "And then we might find a boy who can push you in your cart and we could keep it all secret between us."

"I would like that," he said slowly, his eyes dreamy. "Will you come and talk to me every day?"

"What will Mrs. Medlock think?" Mary asked.

"She will do what I tell her," he said. "And I will tell her that I want you to come and talk to me. I am glad you came."

"So am I," said Mary. "I will come as often as I can, but I will have to look every day for the way into the garden."

"Yes, you must," he said.

"I have been here a long time and you look tired," Mary said. "Shall I go now?"

"I wish you would stay until I go to sleep," he said shyly.

"Shut your eyes," Mary said. "I will do what my Ayah used to do in India. I will pat your hand and sing something quite low." And so she did.

"That is nice," he murmured. When she looked again, he was asleep. She got up, took her candle, and crept away without making a sound.

CHAPTER 13

The Young Rajah

It caused quite a stir when the household found out that Mary knew the secret of young Colin. Martha stared at her in wide-eyed amazement when she learned Colin actually liked Mary and had been pleasant to her.

"Is Colin a hunchback?" Mary asked. "He didn't look like one."

"He isn't yet," Martha said. "But he has never been strong. Mother says he won't get strong by lying on his back looking at picture books in a dark house all day."

"He needs to go out in the garden," Mary said. "It did me good."

Suddenly a bell rang. Martha scurried out to see who needed her. She came straight back to announce that Colin wanted Mary to visit.

Mary hurried to his room. She found a bright fire on the hearth. Colin sat up on his sofa in a velvet dressing gown, surrounded by beautiful books. A spot of color brightened each of his cheeks.

"I've been thinking about you all morning," he said.

"And I've been thinking about you," Mary said. "Martha was terribly afraid when she heard that I'd met you. She thinks Mrs. Medlock might fire her."

"Go and tell Martha to come here," he ordered.

When Martha came in, she was trembling. "I want Mary to visit me," Colin said. "And you are only doing what I want. If Mrs. Medlock tried to send you away, I would send her away!"

"Thank you, sir," Martha bobbed a nervous curtsy and Colin sent her away. He spotted Mary looking at him.

"Why do you look at me like that?" he asked.

"I was thinking about a boy I once saw in India. He was a rajah with rubies and emeralds stuck all over him. He spoke to people just as you spoke to Martha. And I was thinking you are very much like that young rajah and very different from Dickon."

"Who is Dickon?" Colin asked.

"He is Martha's brother," Mary said. "He can charm foxes and squirrels and birds with his flute. They come and listen to him. He says he knows their ways like he was a wild creature himself."

Colin leaned back and commanded that she tell him more about Dickon. She described all the creatures Dickon had told her about on the moor.

"The moor?" Colin said, wide-eyed. "But it's such a great, bare, dreary place!"

"It's the most beautiful place," Mary insisted. "Lovely things grow on it and it's full of creatures building homes and raising families. I've never been there really, but when Dickon talks about it, you feel as if you were there."

"You never see anything if you are ill," Colin complained.

"You can't if you stay in your room," Mary agreed.

"I couldn't go on the moor," he snapped.

"You might, sometime."

"How can I, when I'm going to die?" he said. "And they wish I would."

Mary crossed her arms and frowned. "If they wished it, then I wouldn't just because of that."

"That's what the grand doctor from London said. He said that I could live if I made up my mind to do it."

"Then I think you should," Mary said. "And I think you should meet Dickon. When he talks so much of living things, you couldn't want to die at all. He'll stuff you full of living with his stories."

"Tell me some," Colin said.

And so they passed the time with Mary talking of Dickon. And they looked through Colin's lovely picture books for glimpses of the animals Mary described. They enjoyed themselves so much they forgot about the time.

Soon, they were laughing quite loudly over Ben and his robin. Colin sat up so straight that Mary just knew he had forgotten all about his weak back.

In the midst of laughing, the door opened.

Colin's doctor stood in the doorway and stared. Mrs. Medlock stood beside him and seemed quite ready to fall down from the shock.

"What is this?" the doctor asked.

Colin slipped back into his rajah tone and introduced the doctor to Mary. "She must come and talk to me whenever I call for her," he said.

"Well, don't get too excited," the doctor said helplessly.

"I will get much more excited if she is kept away," Colin warned. And with that, the matter was settled. Colin called for tea, which shocked Mrs. Medlock again. He even ate an entire muffin while Mary told him more stories of the young rajah.

Colin's Temper

After another week of rain, the high arch of blue sky appeared again. Though she had missed the secret garden and Dickon, Mary had enjoyed her time with Colin. They talked and laughed and read to each other from Colin's lovely books. After hearing her stories, Colin said he was certain he would not mind if Dickon looked at him.

"He is an animal charmer," Colin said. "And I am a boy animal!"

Colin and Mary laughed and laughed at that. Mary decided to bring Dickon to meet Colin as soon as she could. So on the first morning that it was sunny again, Mary raced outside.

"It's warm! It's warm!" she cried skipping along the paths.

Everywhere she looked, something had changed. The grass was greener and things stuck up everywhere. The trees were full of buds and so were the bushes. When she reached the secret garden, she found Dickon already there with a crow on his shoulder and a fox cub circling his feet.

"This is Captain," he said, introducing the fox. "And this here's Soot."

Neither animal seemed the least bit afraid of Mary. Together they wandered through the secret garden to see the signs of spring. A whole clump of crocuses burst into purple and orange and gold. Mary bent down and kissed them.

They saw that the robin now had a mate and a nest, so they stayed well away. Dickon said creeping too close to a nest can spoil a friendship with a bird.

Mary told Dickon all about Colin and asked what he thought about sharing the secret of the garden. He thought about it a bit, then said, "I believe if we brought him here, he wouldn't be watching for lumps to grow on his back, he'd be watching the buds and the creatures."

"I thought the same," Mary said excitedly. "I think we must help make him well."

Because there was so much to do in the garden and so many plans to make, Mary was quite late in returning to the house. Martha greeted her, all flustered.

"Colin has gone into his tantrums because you didn't come see him," Martha said in a rush.

Mary's lips pinched together. She was not going to be bullied by an ill-tempered boy. She marched straight to his room where he lay in his bed.

"Why didn't you get up?" she asked.

"I did," he snapped. "But you didn't come, so I made them put me back to bed."

"I was working in the garden with Dickon," she said.

"He can't come anymore if he keeps you from seeing me."

Mary's eyes opened very wide in surprise, then narrowed. "If you send Dickon away, I'll never come into this room again."

"You'll have to if I want you!" Colin cried.

"No, Mr. Rajah, I will not," Mary announced. "And if they drag me, they cannot make me talk to you. Not when you're being a rude and selfish boy!"

"You're selfish!" he roared. "Get out of my room!"

"I'm going and I won't come back! And I was going to tell you lovely stories about this morning, but you'll never ever hear them now!" Mary stomped out of the room.

She found Colin's nurse in the hall laughing. "At least you gave him something to have a tantrum about," the nurse said.

Mary stormed back to her room, but soon felt a bit sorry for Colin. *I'll go back if he asks me nicely,* she decided before she went to bed. She woke in the middle of the night to the most horrible shrieking. Mary knew at once that it must be Colin having a tantrum.

As she listened to the screams, she could understand why they frightened everyone. She was afraid of the sounds, and afraid for Colin. But as the shrieks continued, she soon became angry.

"He ought to be stopped!" she cried.

So Mary hopped out of bed and stomped to Colin's room. The nurse stepped aside as Mary stormed past. She slapped his door open with her hand and ran across the room to the bed.

"You stop!" she shouted. "Stop it. You'll scream yourself to death if you don't. And I wish you would. I hate that screaming. And I hate you."

Colin had never ever been shouted at, and he turned to her in shocked silence. His face looked dreadful, white and red and swollen.

"If you scream again," Mary said, "I'll scream too and I can scream louder than you can. I'll scare you with my screaming!"

"I can't stop," he gasped. "I can't. I felt the lump on my back. I felt it."

"You did not," she snapped, then called. "Nurse, nurse, come here and show me his back this minute!"

The nurse rushed in, willing to do anything for this girl who had made the screaming stop. Mary peered at Colin's back, looking over every inch. It was a thin back but straight.

"There are no lumps here except backbone lumps," Mary said. "If you weren't so thin, you wouldn't feel those either. My backbone stuck out too until I played outside and got fatter."

"I didn't know," the nurse said. "I didn't know he thought he had a lump. I could have told you that your back was straight. You just need to sit up more so it can grow strong."

"Really?" Colin asked weakly.

"Yes, sir."

"You must come outside with Dickon and me," Mary said. "We'll play and the fresh air will make you fat."

"I'll go out with you, Mary," Colin said, still hiccupping a bit from his tantrum. "I do so want to see Dickon. I think if I go out with you, I shall live to grow up!"

So Mary sat beside Colin and told him about Dickon and his fox and crow until the boy grew drowsy. Then she stroked his hand and sang to him. And Colin fell asleep.

CHAPTER 15

The Secret

Having been awake so long in the night, Mary slept late the next morning. Martha told Mary that Colin had asked her to please come see him before going outside.

"Think of him saying *please*! Will you go to see him, Miss? You've done him a world of good already," Martha pleaded.

Mary put her hat on to go outside, but ran to Colin's room first. He was in bed and his face was pale with dark circles around his eyes.

"I'm glad you came," he said. "My head aches. Are you going somewhere?"

"I won't be long," she promised. "I'm going to Dickon, but I'll be back. It's something about the secret garden."

Colin's whole face brightened. "Oh, I dreamed about the garden last night. I'll think about my dream until you come back."

In five minutes, Mary was with Dickon in their garden. The fox and crow were with him, and he'd brought two tame squirrels as well.

"I came over on the pony this morning," he said. "Jump is a good fellow. And these two insisted upon riding in my pockets. This here is Nut, and this is Shell."

Mary and Dickon sat down in the grass and Mary told him about Colin's tantrum. She also told him about the fancy Colin had taken to the idea of the garden and to Dickon.

"The poor lad shut up in the house. I'd scream a bit, too," Dickon said. "We must bring him out here."

"Perhaps, you could come in and visit him?" Mary said.

"Today?" Dickon asked.

Mary thought a moment and shook her head. "Not today. He's a bit wobbly from the night. Perhaps tomorrow."

With that agreed, Mary rushed back in to see Colin while Dickon worked in the garden. "You smell like flowers and fresh things," Colin said when he saw her.

"It's the wind from the moor," she answered. There was so much to talk about and it seemed as if Colin could never hear enough of Dickon, Captain, Soot, Nut, Shell, and the pony Jump.

"I wish I was friends with things," Colin said at last. "But I'm not. I never had anything to be friends with. I can't bear people."

Mary nodded wisely. "I used to feel like that. I hated people. Ben Weatherstaff said it was because I was cross like him."

"But I like you," Colin said. "And I like Dickon, even though I haven't seen him."

"Can I tell you a secret?" Mary asked, catching hold of both his hands. "Can I trust you for sure?"

"Yes," Colin whispered.

"Dickon is coming to see you tomorrow and he's bringing his creatures."

"Oh! Oh!" Colin cried out in delight.

"But that's not all," she whispered. "I found the secret garden. I've been inside."

"Oh Mary!" he cried out, nearly sobbing. "Shall I see it?"

"Of course, don't be silly," she said. "We'll bring you in, because I know I can trust you now. It's our secret garden, and it will make you well. I know it will!"

CHAPTER 16

Dickon Has Come!

Colin's doctor came to see him the morning after his tantrum, as he always did. He arrived in late afternoon, fully expecting to find Colin ready to break into sobs.

"That boy will break a blood vessel in one of those fits someday," he muttered as he bustled toward Mrs. Medlock.

"You'll hardly believe your eyes when you see him," the housekeeper said. "Mary Lennox flew at him like a cat last night. She did what none of us dare to do. Come and see the result."

The doctor found Colin sitting up very straight on his sofa. He was looking at a picture in a garden book and talking to Mary. When they saw the doctor, they fell silent.

"I'm sorry to hear you were ill last night," the doctor said.

"I'm better now," Colin said. "Tomorrow Dickon will visit me, and we're going to go out into the gardens."

The doctor looked alarmed. "You mustn't tire yourself or go out if it's chilly."

"Fresh air won't tire me," Colin said in his rajah voice. "My cousin knows how to take care of me, and Dickon will help."

The doctor knew Dickon, as did most everyone in the area. "Well, you should be safe with Dickon. He's as strong as a moor pony."

"And he's trusty," Mary said, putting on the Yorkshire accent that Dickon and Martha used. "He's the trustiest lad in Yorkshire."

The doctor laughed aloud. He'd never made such a short stay after a tantrum. He was nearly ready to believe that Mary was magic.

That night Colin slept soundly and insisted upon getting out of bed as soon as he woke.

When Mary ran in, he called out, "You've been out! You have that nice smell of leaves."

She had been running, and her hair was loose and windblown. "Spring has come," Mary said. "It has. Dickon says so."

"Has it?" Colin asked.

"Yes!" Mary cried. She ran to the window and flung it open. "Smell it! That's fresh air. Take long breaths. Dickon says that's what makes him strong."

Colin did as she told him, breathing deeply until he felt certain something new and wonderful was happening inside him.

"Dickon found a newborn lamb, and he's brought it with him," Mary said, leaning close. "And he's coming here!"

Colin called the nurse at once and insisted that Dickon be sent to his room the very second he came. Mary and Colin strained to hear, and finally they caught the faint caw of Dickon's crow.

Dickon came in, smiling his nicest smile. The newborn lamb lay in his arms, and the little red fox trotted by his side. Nut sat on his left shoulder and Soot on his right. Shell's head and paws peeped out of his coat pocket.

Colin stared but Dickon was so friendly and calm that Colin soon forgot to be shy. Dickon laid the lamb in Colin's lap and showed him how to feed it from the bottle he'd brought. After its belly was full, the lamb snuggled into Colin's lap.

Soot flew solemnly in and out through the open window. The squirrels dashed out to the big trees outside and ran up and down the trunks. Captain curled up on the rug and fell asleep.

The children looked at pictures of gardens in Colin's books and talked of plans for the secret garden.

"I am going to see it," Colin whispered.

"Aye," Mary said in her put-on Yorkshire accent. "And we must not lose time about it."

I Shall Live Forever
and Ever

They had to wait more than a week to actually get Colin out of doors since the weather turned cool suddenly. The friends passed the time planning. Dickon spent a part of each visit telling of all the creatures bustling about the moor.

"They have to build their homes fresh every year," Dickon explained. "So they fair scuffle to get them done."

Finally, a warm day dawned and Colin called the head gardener to his room. He announced that all the gardeners must stay out of sight as the children walked. He would not have anyone stare at him.

"Very good, sir," replied Mr. Roach.

The young rajah waved his hand and said, "You have my permission to go."

"Very good, sir," Mr. Roach said solemnly, though he burst into laughter as soon as he got into the corridor. He decided that young Colin was like the entire royal family rolled into one.

The strongest footman in the house carried Colin downstairs and put him in his wheeled-chair, then quickly left. Dickon pushed the chair slowly and Mary walked beside.

"There are so many sounds of singing and humming," Colin said, his eyes huge. Not a human creature caught sight of them as they rolled along the paths. Finally, they reached the ivied walls.

"This is it," Mary whispered. She pointed out where the robin showed her the key and where the ivy covered the door. She opened the door and Dickon pushed him in with one strong, steady, splendid push.

Colin gasped and looked around. A fair green veil of tender little leaves seemed to cover everything. Here and there splashes of gold and purple and white burst forth. A pink glow of color crept into Colin's cheeks.

"I shall get well!" he cried out. "I shall! And I shall live forever and ever and ever!"

Mary and Dickon worked about the garden as Colin watched. They brought him things to look at and hold. The robin flashed by with a worm in its beak and Dickon pointed.

"He's taking his lady a bit of dinner. I believe I could use a bit of dinner myself."

Colin sent Mary to ask for a hamper of food so they could eat in the garden. They had hot tea and buttered crumpets. Dickon's animals joined them and enjoyed the food as well.

"I don't want this day to go," Colin said. "But we'll come back every good day."

"And you'll get so much fresh air that you'll get fat and strong like me," Mary said.

"Before long, you'll be walking around here and digging just like us," Dickon said.

"Do you think so?" Colin asked, his eyes wide.

"You've got legs don't you?" Dickon said.

"Yes," Colin said. "But I've never walked on them. Though the doctor in London said there was nothing wrong with them."

Suddenly, in the midst of their chat, Ben Weatherstaff's head peeked over the wall. "I knew I heard voices," he cried, shaking his fist. "It's not allowed. This was her garden and you shouldn't be tromping around in it."

Then Colin sat up very straight in his chair and demanded. "Do you know who I am?"

Ben seemed to notice him for the first time. "Aye, you have your mother's eyes. But I heard you were a cripple."

"I'm not a cripple," Colin said furiously. "I'll show you I'm not!" The strength that Colin usually poured into tantrums ran through him. He swung his legs out of his chair.

Dickon ran to his side. And Mary gripped

her hands tightly together. "He can do it. He can do it. He can," she said over and over.

Colin stood upright as straight as an arrow with Dickon at his side to catch him if he wobbled. "Look at me!"

"Well, the lies folks tell," Ben said.

"I am the master of the house when my father is away," Colin said. "I command you to keep this moment secret. Now come down here."

So Ben came down from the ladder and walked around to enter by the door. Mary explained how the robin had helped her with the key and the door.

"I believe magic sent the robin," Mary said.

Ben looked at Colin, who stood straight and still. "That could be, lass."

"I'm going to walk and dig," Colin said. "Just as you said, Dickon."

Ben chuckled and asked, "Would you like to plant something? I could get a rose in a pot."

"Go and get it!" Colin cried as Dickon helped him sit. He began to dig in the dirt. When he grew tired, Dickon finished the hole for him.

Ben brought a rose in a pot from the greenhouse. "Here, lad," he said. "Set it in place in your dear mother's garden."

Colin's thin white hands shook, but he set the rose in the hole. Then, he held it while old Ben made the earth firm around it.

"It's planted," Colin called at last.

And the sun set on that strange afternoon with Colin standing on his own feet next to his own rose, laughing.

CHAPTER
18

Magic

When Colin finally returned to the house, he was met by the footman and a very worried doctor. "You should not have stayed so long," the doctor fretted. "You'll overexert yourself."

"I'm not tired at all," Colin said. "I'll go out in the morning and the afternoon from now on."

"I'm not sure I can allow that," the doctor said.

"It would not be wise to try and stop me," Colin said with a glare.

Even Mary was taken aback by what a little brute Colin could be. "I'm rather sorry for the doctor," Mary said after the man had left. "It must be horrible to have to be polite to a boy who is always rude."

"Am I rude?" Colin asked, his voice curious.

"If he were a slapping sort of man," Mary said, "he might have slapped you."

"He wouldn't dare," Colin said.

In the months that followed, the garden truly seemed magical. The green things grew bigger and stronger and so did Colin. Ben came most days, and he pointed out which things in the garden were the favorite of Colin's mother.

Colin had always hated hearing about his mother, since he believed her death made his father hate him. But he found that he didn't mind hearing about her favorite flowers and the places where she loved to sit.

The seeds they planted grew and flowered as spring crept toward summer. The children soon knew every inch, every plant, every creature of the garden. There was no end of things for them to explore and talk about.

Then one day, Colin announced that Mary, Dickon, and Ben must line up like soldiers. He told them he planned a scientific experiment to see if the magic were truly real.

"I'm going to make scientific discoveries when I am grown," Colin said. "So I must begin now. I will call the magic and you must call it with me. And we will see if the magic can make me as strong as Dickon."

"Aye, aye, sir," Ben agreed.

"We will do it every day," Colin said. "Like a drill." Then he looked anxiously at his troops. "Do you think the experiment will work?"

Ben smiled warmly. "Aye, that I do."

So each day, they gathered as Colin cried, "The magic is in me! The magic is making me strong."

And each day, his troops agreed with him.

"It is making me stronger," Colin said one morning as he reached high toward the sky.

"What will the doctor say?" Mary said.

"He mustn't know," Colin said. "I want it to be a secret until my father comes home. I want him to know first. I will walk up to him just like any boy and show that I will live to be a man."

"He will think it's a dream," Mary said.

Colin smiled at the thought that his father would no longer find it difficult to look at him. And if the magic were very strong, he might even love Colin a little. But that idea was too big to say aloud.

◦◦◦◦◦◦

As summer came to the secret garden, Colin grew healthier. It became harder to keep his secret. If the doctor knew Colin could walk, he would surely write to his father with the news.

Colin didn't want his father to know until he stood before him. So, Colin had to complain and whimper, even if he didn't feel a bit like it. He tried to act helpless as the footman put him in the chair each day. He even tried having a tantrum once, but he found he really wasn't very good at it anymore.

The thing that was hardest to hide was his appetite. Now, Colin ate every bit of food before him and sometimes asked for more. How could anyone think him sickly with his appetite?

"Your appetite is improving very much, Master Colin," the nurse said one day. "I must talk to the doctor about it."

"How she stared at you," Mary whispered when the nurse had bustled out.

"I won't have her finding out," Colin said. "But I can't help eating so much. I'm so hungry."

They asked Dickon what they ought to do. He suggested that he might bring food from home that they could eat in the garden.

"But I'll have to let Mum in on the secret," he said. "Or else she'll not spare it."

Mary and Colin agreed that Mrs. Sowerby could know the secret. Mary sent her allowance each week to help with the cost of the food.

Mrs. Sowerby sent warm currant buns, fresh milk, and roasted potatoes. The children ate until they were so full, Colin could easily turn down the food he was brought in his room.

The nurse worried so much that she called the doctor to look at Colin. "I am sorry to hear you're not eating," he said. "That will not do."

"I told you it was an unhealthy appetite," Colin whined. "I'm certain I am sick again." He didn't look sick with his rosy complexion and bright eyes. The doctor left, totally confused.

The only lag in Colin's magical healing came on rainy days when they couldn't get into the garden and didn't dare exercise in his room. It was Mary who thought of the solution for that.

"This house has nearly a hundred rooms that no one goes into," she said. "We could explore them and run and run. We would only have to take your chair and insist no one come looking for us."

Colin's face lit up. "That's nearly as good as a secret garden!"

So Colin called for his chair and Mary wheeled him far from the used part of the house. Then he hopped from the chair and the children ran through the halls. They looked at portraits and played with the ivory elephants. They found the mouse family had grown up and left the velvet pillow.

When they finally returned to his room, the two children were so hungry they ate all of the meal laid out for them. Then Colin called for a servant to remove a bit of rose-colored curtain that hung from the wall. Under it, a portrait of a bright-eyed woman looked out at them, laughing.

"That's my mother," Colin said. "I didn't like to look at her, but now I do. We laugh so much now, that I like to think of her laughing, too."

"You look much like her," Mary said. "Like her ghost made into a boy."

Colin thought about that. "If I were her ghost, my father would be fond of me."

"Do you want him to be fond of you?" Mary asked.

"Yes," Colin said. "If he were fond of me, I could tell him about the magic and he wouldn't be so sad anymore."

It's Mother!

Not long after their ramble in the old house, Colin was digging in the secret garden when he was struck by a sense of knowing. He stood and stretched himself out to his fullest height and threw his arms out.

"Look at me," he cried to his friends. "I'm well. I'm truly well." The joy rushed through him and made him laugh.

"That you are," Dickon agreed.

"I want to celebrate," Colin said. "I feel as if I want to shout out something thankful."

"We could sing," Dickon said. "Mother says she believes the skylarks sing thanks when they get up in the morning."

"If she says that, it must be right," Colin said. "You begin and we'll sing what you do."

So Dickon launched into a simple song of thanks and then everyone joined in to sing with him. As the last note hung in the air, Colin stared across the garden, startled by what he saw. "Who is coming?"

Dickon turned to follow his gaze. "It's Mother!" Dickon raced to her at a run and soon Colin and Mary joined him. Colin held out his hand shyly.

"Eh, dear lad," she said.

"Are you surprised because I am so well?" Colin asked.

"Aye, that I am," she said, her eyes misty. "Also, you are so very like your mother that it made my heart jump."

"Do you think it will make my father like me?" Colin asked.

"Aye, for sure, dear lad," she answered, giving his shoulder a quick pat. "He must come home. He must see that there is no lad in Yorkshire with a straighter back or stronger legs."

Then she turned and put both hands on Mary's shoulders. "And you too! You're as hearty as my own Elizabeth Ellen. Martha told me your mother was said to be a pretty woman. You'll be a rose when you grow up."

Mrs. Sowerby went around their garden and learned every story of it from them. Colin walked on one side of her and Mary on the other. Each of them looked into her rosy face and thought her the perfect sort of mother to have.

At last Colin told her about the magic of the garden. "Do you believe in magic?" he asked.

"That I do, lad," she said. "I have not called it by that name, but the name doesn't matter, only the wondrous result."

She had packed a basket with her and they sat down to a regular feast with as much laughing as food in it. She was full of fun and made them laugh at all sorts of odd things.

"We laugh nearly all the time when we're together," Colin said. "It is very hard to seem sick when you're laughing."

"I can see you do have a good bit of play acting to do," Mrs. Sowerby said. "But you won't have to keep it up much longer. I am sure Mr. Craven will be home soon."

"Do you think he will?" Colin asked. "I think of different ways to show him. I'm not sure which way is best, but I know I want to be the one to show him. No one must tell him."

Mrs. Sowerby smiled. "I would like to see his face, lad."

Then they planned a visit to her cottage, for they knew they wanted to spend more time together and meet all of the children.

"I wish you were my mother," Colin said shyly. "As well as Dickon's."

Mrs. Sowerby hugged him then. "Eh, dear lad! Your own mother is in this very garden, I do believe. She could not keep away from you. And your father will be home soon. He must."

In the Garden

Colin's father had traveled far and wide since the day he saw Miss Mary in his study and said she might have her "bit of earth." He had gone to some of the most beautiful places in Europe, but no matter where he went, he carried the burden of his sadness.

Then one day in the Austrian Tyrol, he gazed into a clear stream that ran merrily through luscious damp greenness. He noticed blue forget-me-nots growing along the bank and remembered how he had looked at such things years before. And as he let the smallest bit of beauty sink into him, he felt a little less miserable.

What he didn't know was that the very moment when he felt a little of his misery slide away, a little boy far away was shouting, "I am going to live forever and ever and ever."

As the golden summer moved toward autumn, Archibald Craven found himself seeing more and more of what was beautiful in the world. He walked far and wide so that he could see more and more. He began to sleep better.

One night, he had a dream of his beautiful Lilias in her garden. She was calling him to come to her in the garden. And the next day, he found the oddest note had come for him to the villa where he was staying.

Dear Sir,

I once spoke to you upon the moor about Miss Mary. I make bold to speak again. Please, sir, I think you would be very glad if you come home. And I think your lady would ask you to come home if she were here.

Your Obedient Servant,
Susan Sowerby

Mr. Craven read the note several times. "Yes," he said softly. "Yes, I'll go at once."

In a few days, he was in Yorkshire again. On the long railway trip, he'd fretted about his boy. Could Mrs. Sowerby have been gently coaxing him home because his son was dying?

"What have I been doing these ten years?" he said quietly to himself. "What have I been thinking?"

The drive across the wonderfulness of the moor was a soothing thing. He looked across the beauty of the land and he saw it.

"We loved this place," he whispered. And suddenly, he was desperate to walk in the garden that his wife had loved so much. "I will try to find the key," he murmured. "I must see inside."

When he arrived at the house, the servants noticed right away that he seemed different. He did not wander past them, but asked briskly for his son.

"Is he…worse?" he asked Mrs. Medlock.

"Sir," she said. "Neither the doctor nor the nurse can rightly make him out. His ways are so peculiar, more than ever before. His appetite and the look of him. And he insists on being out of doors!"

"Where is he now?" Mr. Craven asked.

"In the garden," she said. "He's always in the garden. No one is allowed look at him when he goes in the garden."

"In the garden," Mr. Craven murmured, remembering the odd dream of his wife. He turned and headed out into the gardens, naturally following the route the children took each morning. He felt drawn to the locked door of the garden Lilias had loved. And when he reached it, he started. He heard voices from inside—young voices and laughter.

Mr. Craven pushed away the ivy and found the door open. He heard running feet. Then, with a laugh, a boy burst through the door at full speed, looking behind him as he ran. He dashed almost into Mr. Craven's arms.

He was a tall, handsome boy who glowed with life. He had thick hair that hung over his forehead. He pushed it away as he looked up at Mr. Craven. He had huge, gray eyes with black lashes like fringe and Mr. Craven knew those eyes in an instant. He gasped.

"Father," the boy said, still panting a bit from his run, "I'm Colin. I'm well. The garden did it. There's magic there. I can beat Mary in a race. I'm going to be an athlete."

All the words tumbled over each other like the words of any healthy boy in high excitement. Then he laid his hand on his father's arm. "Aren't you glad, Father? Aren't you glad?"

His father put his hands on both of the boy's shoulders and said, "Take me into the garden, my boy, and tell me all about it."

And so they went in. The garden was wild and bright with autumn gold and scarlet. Late lilies stood together adding their bright white. Late roses climbed everywhere. Mr. Craven looked and looked. "I thought it would be dead," he whispered.

"Mary thought so too, at first," Colin said and Mary nodded in agreement. "But it came alive."

Mr. Craven listened to Colin's story of mystery and magic and wild creatures and half-wild children and secrets that poured from Colin.

"Now it doesn't need to be a secret anymore," Colin said. "Won't it frighten everyone into fits when I walk into the house with you, Father?"

The servants gathered to gape out the windows when the Master of Misselthwaite walked toward them, looking as many of them had never seen him. Colin walked by his side with his head up and his eyes full of laughter, looking as strong and steady as any boy in Yorkshire!